LOVERS IN THE VEIL

A SHORT, OPPOSITES ATTRACT, TAROT, MYTHOLOGY ROMANCE

TAROT FANTASIES
BOOK 11

JAX WILDER

LOVERS IN THE VEIL

Tarot Fantasies Series

Jax Wilder

RAINBOW QUARTZ PUBLISHING

Published by Rainbow Quartz Publishing

Edmonds WA, 98026

ISBN: 978-1-961714-60-1

First Edition: 2024

Cover design by Miranda Townsend Interior design by Miranda Townsend

Tarot Card description by Lorelai Hamilton from the book Teenage Tarot – used with permission.

Library of Congress Cataloging-in-Publication Data has been applied for.

This book is a work of fiction. Names, characters, places, and incidents are either the product of the author's imagination or used fictitiously. Any resemblance to actual events, locales, or persons, living or dead, is entirely coincidental.

For permissions or inquiries, please contact Rainbow Quartz Publishing:

rainbowquartzpublishing@gmail.com RQPublishing.com

This one is for all the artist.
We all need a little muse some times.

Jax Wilder

6. THE LOVERS

"You have the power to choose who you want to be with and who you want to surround yourself with," The Lovers.

KEY WORDS AND PHRASES: UNION AND PARTNERSHIP

Love and relationships
Harmony and balance
Mutual attraction and connection
Choices and decisions
Soulmates and deep connections
Emotional fulfillment
Commitment and devotion
Alignment of values and beliefs
Integration of opposites

The Lovers card is a beautiful scene. There is a couple standing, totally in love and connected. They're soulmates and in perfect balance with one another. The Lovers card is about relationships and connections. There is someone who gets you and understands you completely.

The Lovers card is also about making choices. You have options in life, and you have the power to choose not just who you want to be with, but who you surround yourself with. Following your heart and doing what feels right to you is key.

—Lorelai Hamilton, author of *Teenage Tarot* and *Tarot Tales & Magic Spells*

VI

THE LOVERS.

CHAPTER
ONE

stared at the sketch in front of me, frustration building in my chest. It was the last card for my new tarot deck, the one I'd been working on for months, but it didn't matter. The excitement, the rush of creating something beautiful, had fizzled out long ago. Now, it felt like I was just going through the motions.

There was a time when every brushstroke felt alive, when the ideas seemed to flow effortlessly from my mind to the page. I thought I could hold on to that feeling forever, back when I first started this deck. Back when love and inspiration were tangled together, back when I'd believed in both.

I could still see the way Ethan used to watch me work, his eyes lit up with admiration as I filled the canvas with color and symbols. But that was years ago. Love faded. So did the art. Now, it felt like a distant memory, and I wasn't sure if I'd ever get it back.

The sunlight streamed through the window, casting a warm glow over my cluttered studio. Outside, the town buzzed with life, but it felt distant, like I was watching it from behind glass. Everyone else was out there living, while I was stuck in here— waiting for something I couldn't quite name.

I sighed, tossing my pencil aside. Maybe I just needed a change of scenery. There was one place I could always go when I felt this restless. The Arcane Room.

When I stepped inside, the familiar smell of incense and herbs hit me, wrapping around me like a comforting hug. The little bell above the door jingled, announcing my arrival. Ms. Vesper was behind the counter, her wild silver hair pulled back loosely as she arranged rows of crystal bottles.

"April," she greeted me with a smile that crinkled the corners of her sharp, bright eyes. "I was wondering when you'd show up."

I managed a small smile back. "Hey, Vesper. Thought I'd stop by. Needed a break."

She eyed me over her glasses. "Still working on that deck, huh? Must be driving you crazy."

"You have no idea." I leaned against the counter, dropping my sketchbook beside me. "I'm almost done, but... something's missing. It doesn't feel right."

She nodded, as if she understood exactly what I meant, and then motioned to the book. "What's the latest card?"

I flipped it open to my most recent sketch. "The Lovers. I've been trying to perfect it."

"The Lovers, huh?" Vesper gave me a sly grin. "And yet, here you are, still looking a bit... unsatisfied."

I groaned. "It's not that. I mean, sure, I haven't exactly had the best luck in that department, but... I don't know. I've been throwing myself into my art because it's the only thing that makes sense. Lately, though, it's like... even that isn't enough."

Art had always been my way of keeping people at arm's length, my safe haven. Relationships? Not so much. I tried, of course. I let people in, but the moment things got serious, I'd bury myself in my work. It was easier that way. But now, even that escape was fading.

She tilted her head, studying me for a long moment. "Sounds like you could use a little insight. Let me give you a reading."

I rolled my eyes. "I think I know the cards well enough, don't you?"

"Then what's the harm?" She smirked, grabbing a nearby deck. "Come on, humor me."

With a resigned sigh, I shuffled the cards and drew one, slapping it face up on the counter. Of course.

"The Lovers," I muttered. "Great. Just what I needed."

Ms. Vesper let out a cackle. "Oh, the irony."

I stared down at the card, the figures entwined in a perfect balance, their connection undeniable. I knew the symbolism by heart, but looking at it now, it felt like a cruel joke. I couldn't remember the last time I felt that kind of connection with anyone.

Ms. Vesper raised an eyebrow. "Maybe the universe is trying to tell you something."

"Or it's just messing with me."

"Maybe." She chuckled softly and moved toward the back of the shop, disappearing behind a curtain. When she returned, she held a steaming cup of tea, the fragrant steam swirling toward me. "Here, drink this. It'll help you relax. You look like you could use it."

I eyed the cup warily. "What is it?"

"Just a blend I make for when people need to unwind." She pushed the cup toward me. "Trust me. You need this."

I hesitated for a moment before taking the cup, the warmth of it comforting against my palms. I trusted Vesper, even if she had a flair for the dramatic. I brought the cup to my lips and took a sip. The tea was sweet and floral, soothing in a way that settled deep in my bones.

"Come with me," Vesper said, leading me toward a small, white room at the back of the shop. It was simple, with a single black leather chaise lounge in the center of the room. "Sit, close your eyes, and just breathe."

I sat down, the tea still warm in my hands, and did as she said. I closed my eyes, focusing on my breath as I drank slowly. I didn't even realize how tense I'd been until the tea started to work its way through me, relaxing my muscles and calming my mind.

"Just let go," Vesper's voice whispered from somewhere in the room. "Let whatever comes, come."

The last sip of tea slid down my throat, and a heavy wave of drowsiness hit me. I leaned back, sinking into the couch. My eyelids grew impossibly heavy, and the world around me began to blur.

And then... nothing.

When I opened my eyes again, the world had changed. I wasn't in the white room anymore.

I was... floating.

I sat up, my breath catching in my throat as I took in the sight around me. I was on an island suspended in the sky, surrounded by swirling clouds and a golden sunset that seemed to stretch forever. Temples and statues stood in the distance, their marble columns glowing in the soft light.

This wasn't real.

But it felt so real.

I stood, my bare feet sinking into the soft, warm

grass, and looked around. Everything here was beautiful—beyond anything I could have imagined. The air was warm, sweet, like the tea I had just finished, and a gentle breeze tugged at my hair.

I wasn't sure how long I stood there, taking it all in, but it felt like time had no meaning in this place.

Then I saw him.

A figure in the distance, walking toward me through the golden light. He moved with grace, his dark hair catching the light as he drew closer. And when his eyes met mine, something inside me stirred, like a forgotten memory suddenly surfacing.

He smiled, and my heart skipped a beat.

"Welcome," he said, his voice low and smooth. "I've been waiting for you."

CHAPTER
TWO

"You've been waiting for me?" I asked, my voice dripping with skepticism. "How is that possible when, up until about thirty seconds ago, I didn't even know I was coming here?"

The man in front of me smiled, a slow, confident curl of his lips. His gaze swept over me, warm and intense, as if he'd known me for years. His dark eyes seemed to drink me in, and the air between us crackled with something electric—something I wasn't sure I was ready for.

"I have my ways," he said, his voice low and sultry. "And when you appeared here, I knew you were the one I'd been waiting for."

I couldn't help the laugh that bubbled up. "Really? That's a bit much, don't you think?"

His smile deepened, and he stepped closer.

"You'll come to realize that I never exaggerate when it comes to love and desire." His hand brushed lightly against my arm, sending a shiver down my spine. "My name is Eros."

I raised an eyebrow. "Eros? As in the god of love?" My voice was dry, and I crossed my arms, unimpressed despite the flutter in my stomach.

His smile didn't falter. "Who else would I be? My mother, Aphrodite, would be quite displeased if you thought otherwise."

I blinked. "Who names their kid Eros?"

"A goddess, of course."

I couldn't help but roll my eyes, but before I could reply, he gestured toward the expansive island around us, a glint of amusement in his eyes. "Come, let me show you around my home. Consider yourself my guest here. Whatever your heart desires can be yours."

I hesitated for a moment, still trying to wrap my head around the absurdity of the situation. But something about the way he looked at me—like he was seeing parts of me I didn't even know existed—made me curious. And a little more than intrigued.

"Alright," I said, slipping my arm through his. "Show me."

He grinned, that playful look never leaving his face. "Good choice. Just, uh, try to stay away from the edge." He nodded toward the edge of the island, which seemed to drop off into a swirling mass of clouds. "It's a long way down."

We walked arm in arm, and I couldn't shake the strange comfort I felt in his presence. As we made our way across the floating island, I took in the beauty of it all—the golden light of the sunset, the vibrant colors of the flowers that bloomed everywhere, and the peaceful hum of the place, like it existed just for us.

Eros led me to a temple, its tall marble columns covered in a rainbow of flowers. They seemed to spill from the ground, climbing the stone walls, filling the air with a sweet, intoxicating fragrance. Inside, the light softened, casting a golden glow over everything. In the center of the temple was a pool of crystal-clear water, its surface shimmering in the soft light.

I looked around, feeling like I had stepped into a dream. "Are we... alone here?"

Eros turned to me, his dark eyes sparkling with mischief. "Do you want to be?"

I blinked. "What kind of answer is that?"

"The kind where, if you wanted us to be joined by others..." He snapped his fingers, and suddenly, the temple was filled with people—muscled men and curvy, beautiful women, their bodies barely covered by scraps of cloth. They moved with grace, some lounging by the pool, others dancing slowly to a music I couldn't hear. The air was thick with sensuality.

I stumbled over my words, my eyes wide. "What —how did—?"

Eros snapped his fingers again, and in an instant, the temple was empty, save for us. He gave me a devilish grin. "We're in the Arcane Room. Anything is possible here."

"Anything?" I asked, my voice barely above a whisper.

He stepped closer, his gaze locking onto mine. "Anything," he murmured.

My stomach growled, breaking the spell between us. I laughed awkwardly, pressing a hand to my belly. "Well, I'm suddenly a bit hungry."

With another snap of his fingers, a golden table appeared in front of us, laden with the most beautiful spread of fruits, cheeses, and delicacies I'd ever seen —grapes, strawberries, watermelon, everything fresh and glistening in the golden light. My mouth watered at the sight.

Eros led me to the table, his hand resting lightly on the small of my back. As I reached for a strawberry, my eyes caught sight of the whipped cream, and a sudden, wicked thought crossed my mind. I glanced at Eros, his impossibly attractive figure practically oozing seduction, and a flush crept up my neck.

I dipped a strawberry into the whipped cream,

bringing it to my lips slowly, deliberately. Eros watched me, his dark eyes gleaming with desire.

"I prefer mine with chocolate," he said, his voice low and husky. He dipped a finger into the bowl of chocolate, and before I could react, he gently ran it across my neck. The sensation sent a shock of heat through my body.

Then, he leaned in, his lips brushing against my skin as he licked the chocolate from my neck, his tongue warm and slow. A soft moan escaped me before I could stop it, and my whole body tingled with need. Heat pooled low in my belly, and I found myself breathless, my mind swimming with desire.

Without thinking, I dipped my fingers into the whipped cream and ran them across his neck. I leaned in, licking the sweet, creamy mixture from his skin, savoring the taste of him—warm, salty, utterly intoxicating.

We were lost after that.

I wasn't sure who started it, but soon we were covered in fruit, chocolate, and whipped cream, our bodies sticky and slick as we devoured each other in every way imaginable. Clothes disappeared, tossed aside like afterthoughts as Eros licked and kissed every inch of me, his tongue and lips dragging out moans and gasps I didn't even recognize as mine.

"You taste delightful," he whispered against my skin, his voice sending shivers through me.

My head was spinning, lost in the feel of him, his

body pressed against mine, hard and hot. His mouth found my breasts, dribbling chocolate across them before he licked it clean, his lips closing around my nipples, suckling gently. Heat tugged at my core, and I arched into him, craving more.

I reached for him, my hands shaking as I stripped his pants off, revealing his sculpted body. I dribbled whipped cream across his thighs, down the hard planes of his abs, and licked it up, nipping at his skin as I went. Every touch made him groan, the sound vibrating through me like music.

He caught my mouth in a heated kiss, his hands roaming over my body, and I was gone, completely lost in him. His hands slipped lower, pulling off my panties. I begged him, my voice ragged and desperate. "I want to feel you inside of me."

Eros groaned, slipping a finger inside me, finding me wet and ready. "You're so eager," he murmured in that deep, seductive voice. "So ready for me."

I moaned, arching into him, begging for more. And then he was inside me, his long, thick cock filling me, stretching me, making me gasp at the sensation.

He moved slowly at first, teasing me with every stroke, until I was clawing at his back, moaning loud enough for the sound to echo off the temple walls. The pleasure built inside me, slowly at first, but then it grew, tightening like a coil inside me. I was so close —so close I could hardly breathe.

"More," I begged. "Faster. Harder. Please."

He obliged, his thrusts becoming faster, harder, until I was on the edge of oblivion. And then, finally, I fell, the orgasm tearing through me, making me scream his name as I rode the waves of pleasure in his arms.

CHAPTER
THREE

"Well, that was... unexpected," I said, my voice breathless and still tinged with disbelief. My heart was pounding, my body still humming from the intensity of what had just happened. I blinked up at Eros, who was lying beside me, the satisfied grin of a god etched on his impossibly handsome face.

He chuckled softly, the sound deep and sultry. "Unexpected? Darling, you're in the Arcane Room. Nothing is ever quite what it seems."

I swallowed, trying to shake the feeling of being swept up in something much bigger than myself. I'd never just... hooked up with someone before, especially not someone like him. "I've never done that," I admitted, my voice small. "Just... you know, slept with someone like that. So fast."

Eros propped himself up on one elbow, his dark

eyes gleaming with amusement and something more —something deeper. "You wouldn't be the first to give in to desire with me," he said, his voice a low purr. "I've been with a lot of women. Men. And everyone in between. Love, after all, is for everyone." His smile was playful, but the way he said it, like every word dripped with sex and promise, made my pulse race all over again.

I suddenly felt small, insignificant. Who was I compared to the god of love? It wasn't just about him being a god. It was about me—always feeling like I wasn't enough. Not for my ex, not for anyone. Ethan had loved the idea of me, the artist, the dreamer. But when I faltered, when I struggled, the shine faded. Maybe that's why I threw myself into my work— because art never judged me. But now, standing in front of Eros, I felt every crack in my armor, every insecurity I'd ever tried to hide.

I was just a woman—an artist trying to figure out my life. He was Eros, eternal, perfect, with countless lovers who had probably been far more captivating than I could ever be. The thought hit me like a stone, and I couldn't help the wave of insecurity that washed over me.

Eros's gaze softened, as if he could sense my thoughts. Maybe he could. "Being with someone sexually," he murmured, his voice velvet smooth, "is one thing. But being in love with someone—that's something else entirely." He reached out, trailing a finger down my arm, his touch warm and comforting. "Sex, my dear April, is a beautiful act of pleasure, connection, and desire. But love... love is different. Love is human."

I raised an eyebrow, surprised. "Love is human? But you're the god of love."

His smile was wistful, almost sad. "Yes, I am. But gods are eternal. We love expansively, in ways that transcend time, space, and mortal understanding. But being in love... that's something singularly magical. It's fleeting and fragile, yet powerful beyond measure. It's a fire that burns so brightly it can light up a soul. I never truly understood it before."

He looked at me then, his gaze intense, as if he were seeing something in me that even I didn't know was there. "Until now."

His words took my breath away. There was something so raw in his voice, something that pulled me toward him, even though I wasn't sure I could handle the weight of it. The way he looked at me, like I was the most magical thing in the world, left me both vulnerable and enchanted.

I swallowed hard, trying to push the fluttering in my chest away. "That's... a lot to take in," I managed, my voice shaky. I wasn't used to this kind of intensity, not from someone like him. I felt like I was teetering on the edge of something too deep, too big for me to comprehend.

Desperate to lighten the mood and avoid being

sucked into the gravitational pull of his words, I cleared my throat and changed the subject. "So, uh... what else do you have on this floating island of yours?"

Eros's grin returned, bright and mischievous. "Ah, well. Have you ever sat in a field of bunnies?"

I blinked, caught completely off guard. "Bunnies? Like... rabbits? No. What do you mean?"

"Follow me," he said, standing up and holding a hand out for me, completely unbothered by the fact that we were both still naked.

I hesitated, feeling a wave of self-consciousness wash over me as I stood. But Eros didn't seem to care, and his confidence was infectious. So, I took his hand, and together, we skipped out of the temple and into the sunlight.

We wandered through a field of wildflowers, their vibrant colors dancing in the soft breeze. And then, as if by magic, I saw them. Hundreds—no, thousands—of tiny, fluffy bunnies scattered across the field. It was like a scene from a dream, completely surreal.

"This is insane," I said, laughing despite myself.

Eros chuckled, giving me a playful wink. "Bunnies are sacred animals to me, you know. They represent fertility, abundance, and, of course, a bit of mischief. You could say they're my companions of sorts."

"Companions?" I raised an eyebrow, still grinning. "I had no idea bunnies were so... important to the god of love."

"They're quite special," he said with a smirk. "Besides, who can resist petting a bunny? They're adorable, and so very soft."

I knelt down, my fingers brushing against the fur of one of the rabbits. To my surprise, it was even softer than I imagined, its tiny body warm and gentle against my hand. I laughed again, the absurdity of the moment making me feel lighter. "Okay, I admit, this is pretty magical."

Eros grinned, standing tall against the golden backdrop of the island. "See? Even the simplest things can bring joy." His eyes twinkled as he watched me. "So, what else would you like to see? I've got plenty of tricks up my sleeve."

I stood, brushing wildflower petals off my knees. "Oh, I'm sure you do. But you'll have to show me something really special to top this."

Eros leaned closer, his voice dropping to a seductive whisper. "Oh, April, I've barely begun."

CHAPTER
FOUR

The bunnies vanished like a dream, and before I could even blink, we were floating on a cloud. I gasped, looking down at the soft, billowing surface beneath us. It felt like we were weightless, suspended in the air, cradled by the sky itself. The sensation was intoxicating, like I was drifting in a sea of warmth and light.

I couldn't stop the smile that crept across my lips as the cloud lifted us higher, the breeze soft against my skin. It felt like flying, like being unbound by anything earthly. I couldn't remember the last time I felt like this—light, free. Like the weight of the world wasn't pressing down on me.

Maybe I'd never felt this way before. I was always the one in control, holding the reins tight. Even in my art, every brushstroke, every decision, had to be perfect. But here... with him... I didn't need to control anything. I could just... be.

Eros glanced at me, a knowing grin on his face. "And I didn't even have to prick you with an arrow," he said, his voice smooth and teasing.

The comment sent a ripple of realization through me. I was enamored with him. Completely. There was something about Eros that made me feel seen, like he could peer into the deepest parts of me and still want more. His gaze made my pulse quicken, his presence electrified every nerve in my body.

He moved then, slowly crawling across the cloud toward me, his dark eyes never leaving mine. The intensity in his gaze made me feel vulnerable and powerful all at once, and my breath hitched as he began to trail his lips along my skin.

He started with my feet, his kisses soft but purposeful. Each press of his lips sent tingles racing up my legs. I watched him, mesmerized as he kissed each of my toes, then slowly moved up to my ankles, his breath warm against my skin. His hands caressed my calves, then higher, his lips trailing fire up my legs until he reached my thighs.

A moan escaped me before I could stop it, the electricity in my body sparking as his mouth moved higher, closer to the heat that was building between my legs. He spread my thighs apart, and I was trembling beneath him, completely at his mercy.

Eros looked up at me, his eyes dark with desire.

His voice was low, smooth as honey. "You are every-thing, April Psyche Sullivan. Every part of you is divine." The way he said my name—my full name—made me feel like I was the singular most important thing in the universe. His words were a balm to my insecurities, his gaze telling me I was worthy, wanted, desired.

He pushed my thighs apart further, and his mouth found me, hot and wet, his tongue gliding over my slit. I gasped, my body arching as his nose nudged against my clit. "You taste like honey and wine," he murmured against me, inhaling deeply before licking a long, slow stripe from my entrance to my clit.

I was lost. The sensations that tore through me were too much, too intense, and I couldn't think—could barely breathe. My hands twisted in the soft cloud beneath me, my body writhing under his touch. His tongue flicked over my clit, teasing and drawing moans from my lips. Every nerve in my body was alive, buzzing with pleasure.

He slipped a finger inside me, and I whimpered, my hips rocking against him. I needed more. I couldn't get enough of him. He thrust another finger inside me, his tongue still circling my clit, never letting up. I was losing control, my body moving on its own, my legs trembling as the pleasure coiled tight in my core.

"Eros..." I breathed, my voice barely a whisper.

He groaned, his mouth never leaving my clit as he stretched me with three fingers, each thrust sending shockwaves of pleasure through my body. My breathing became ragged, every muscle tightening, my heart pounding. I could feel the orgasm building inside me, slow and hot, curling and tightening.

"Oh my goddess," I gasped as he found my G-spot, and the pleasure became too much. My body exploded, a rush of liquid squirting out of me as I came harder than I ever had before.

For a moment, I was mortified. That had never happened to me before. "I—oh god—" I stammered, trying to pull away, but Eros was relentless, his lips pressing against my thigh as he whispered, "Oh my sweet goddess, that's your sweet juice."

He licked me clean, his tongue savoring every drop before he kissed his way up my stomach, his hands still caressing my trembling body. His lips found mine, the taste of me still lingering on his tongue as he pressed his body against mine.

I was shaking, my heart still racing as he positioned himself between my legs. His cock, hard and ready, pressed against my entrance, and I moaned softly, feeling the heat of him. He entered me slowly, filling me, stretching me in ways I didn't think were possible.

His thrusts were slow at first, gentle, as he watched my face with a kind of reverence that made my heart swell. His hands roamed over my body, touching every part of me, like he was memorizing the feel of my skin beneath his fingertips.

The pleasure built again, deep within my belly, pulling at every part of me. It was like strings attached to every nerve ending, each one tugging me closer to the edge of something I couldn't name.

"Eros," I gasped, digging my fingers into his back, feeling the muscles ripple under my hands as he thrust harder, faster. The cloud beneath us seemed to vibrate with every movement, and I could feel myself slipping away, lost in the rhythm of his body against mine.

The orgasm came slowly at first, like a wave creeping up the shore, but then it hit me all at once, crashing through me with a force that left me breathless. I screamed his name, my body shaking, my mind completely unraveling as I rode the waves of pleasure, clinging to him.

He didn't stop, his thrusts relentless, and I was floating—literally, figuratively—on cloud nine with him. The world around us faded, and all that mattered was him, and the way he made me feel. Like I was the only thing that mattered.

CHAPTER
FIVE

I opened my eyes slowly, blinking against the golden light filtering through the temple walls. There was a time when I'd wake up feeling numb, like the world had lost its color. After Ethan left, after the love faded, I wasn't sure if I'd ever feel alive again. I had buried myself in my work, in the routine of it all, trying to forget. But now, as I blinked against the golden light, I felt more awake than I had in years. More... alive.

It took a moment for my brain to catch up, to realize that we were no longer on the cloud. Magic. Magic was amazing. I pushed myself up, feeling stronger, more alive, like I had been charged with something electric and powerful.

Eros stood nearby, watching me with that familiar, gentle smile that made my heart skip a beat. "You're back with me," he said softly, stepping closer.

"I was starting to wonder if I'd lost you to the clouds."

I smiled, shaking my head. "I'm stronger now."

"Good," he said, snapping his fingers.

I blinked as a tray appeared before me, loaded with food. Not just any food—my favorite food. Mac and cheese with peas and olives, pizza with pesto sauce and artichokes, bacon, apples, watermelon, pork fried rice, and pad Thai. There was even a little cup of extra olives on the side, just the way I liked it.

I stared at the feast in disbelief. "Not exactly sexy," I muttered, half laughing.

"But it's all your favorites," Eros replied, his voice warm and teasing. "You need sustenance. I want to spoil you."

I looked up at him, raising an eyebrow. "Spoil me with mac and cheese?"

"And olives," he added with a wink. "I want to spend my life making all your favorite foods. And I want to show you the world."

His words sent a shiver down my spine. This wasn't real. This was a dream, wasn't it? I shook my head, trying to remember why I couldn't let myself believe in this. "This is only temporary," I said quietly. "This is just a dream."

Eros's expression softened as he knelt beside me. "It doesn't have to be."

I didn't know what to do with that. My heart raced, my thoughts tangling with the possibilities. I thought about the last time I'd felt this inspired, this alive, and the truth hit me like a punch to the gut. I'd never felt this way before. I'd never been this full of love and passion, so connected to someone that it felt like I was living in pure art, pure emotion.

I looked at the food in front of me, then back at Eros. "I want to create. I want to love. I've never felt this way before."

"Then let yourself have it," he said softly.

I hesitated for a moment, then reached for the mac and cheese. The moment I took the first bite, warmth flooded through me. It wasn't just food—it was comfort, love, joy. Every bite was like a hit of dopamine, filling me with a sense of peace and happiness that I hadn't realized I'd been missing. I looked up at Eros, smiling as he picked up a slice of pizza, offering me a bite.

I took it, laughing as we fed each other like it was the most natural thing in the world. Each bite was an act of love, and with every swallow, I felt my heart expand a little more. I was falling for him, deeper and deeper, and it terrified me. But it also thrilled me.

When we finished, Eros leaned back, watching me with those deep, captivating eyes. "There's something I want to show you."

I wiped my hands on a napkin, curiosity bubbling up inside me. "What is it?"

"You'll see." He stood, offering me his hand, and I took it without hesitation.

He led me out of the temple and into a garden that seemed to stretch on forever, bathed in the soft glow of twilight. The air was warm, carrying the sweet scent of jasmine and wildflowers, and all around us, there were butterflies—thousands upon thousands of them.

Their delicate wings fluttered like whispers in the air, catching the light as they moved. Each one was a masterpiece, a burst of color that shimmered with iridescence. Some were as small as my fingertip, while others were as large as my hand, their wings painted with every shade imaginable—deep blues, fiery oranges, soft pinks, and vibrant yellows. Together, they danced in the air, swirling in mesmerizing patterns like living brushstrokes against the canvas of the sky.

The trees around the garden were draped in vines and blossoms, their branches heavy with the weight of nature's beauty. Butterflies clung to the leaves, clustering in groups, their wings moving in unison, creating a gentle, rhythmic pulse that seemed to blend with the sound of the distant breeze. The grass beneath my feet was impossibly soft, dotted with glowing flowers that opened and closed in response to the butterflies' touch, adding to the sense of enchantment that surrounded us.

My breath caught in my throat as I stepped forward, feeling the weight of the magic in the air. I extended my arms, and to my amazement, the butterflies began to drift toward me, their delicate wings brushing against my skin like the softest silk.

They landed on my arms, my shoulders, my hair, their tiny feet tickling me as they perched. I felt their warmth, their life force, humming through me. It was as if the entire garden had come alive just for this moment—just for me.

I turned in a slow circle, feeling the gentle weight of them. And then, something even more incredible happened. I felt a lightness at my back, a warmth spreading between my shoulder blades.

I glanced over my shoulder just in time to see a pair of wings unfurling from my back. They weren't painful. They weren't even solid, exactly. They were made of light, shimmering and magical, as if they were born from the butterflies themselves.

I gasped, feeling my heart race as I flapped the wings experimentally. They responded to my every thought, and suddenly, I was rising from the ground. I soared into the air, spinning with the butterflies, feeling weightless and free.

It was a perfect moment. Something I could only ever imagine, and yet here I was, living it. My heart swelled with joy, and for the first time in what felt like forever, I let myself truly fly.

I spun in the air, the butterflies swirling around me, the colors blurring into a whirlwind of beauty. It was everything I'd ever dreamed of, everything I'd ever wanted. And as I descended, coming back down to the ground, tears filled my eyes.

I landed gently, and Eros was there, waiting for me. But he didn't approach. He let me have the moment to myself, watching as I wiped the tears from my cheeks.

"I've never..." I whispered, my voice thick with emotion. "I've never felt so inspired."

Eros stepped forward, his hand reaching out to cup my cheek. "That's because you were made for this. You were made to create, to love. Let yourself be everything you were meant to be."

I closed my eyes, leaning into his touch, feeling the overwhelming sense of love and inspiration well up inside me. All I wanted to do was make art. All I wanted to do was love this incredible man for as long as I could.

CHAPTER
SIX

Eros led me through a series of stone hallways, their walls cool and smooth beneath my fingertips. The air was fragrant with something sweet and floral, and my heart pounded in my chest, anticipation blooming as we walked. I could feel his presence behind me, so close that the warmth of him brushed against my skin. The sexual energy between us was undeniable, crackling in the air.

When we stepped into the garden, my breath caught. It was like nothing I had ever seen before.

The sky was a rainbow—literally. Hues of violet, cerulean, and blush pink swirled together in a riot of color, colors I had never imagined. The soft light bathed the entire garden, making the leaves and flowers shimmer. The plants themselves were impossibly lush, draped in blossoms of every kind—roses, lavender, orchids—and there, in the center, stood a fountain. A marble cupid, exquisitely carved, poised with his bow drawn, shooting a stream of crystalline water into the air. The sound of it was like music, a soft, melodic rhythm that calmed and inspired me all at once.

And surrounding the fountain were several large easels, each canvas blank and waiting. Every kind of art supply imaginable was laid out for me—acrylics, oils, pastels, charcoals, brushes of every size, palettes brimming with paint in every shade. It was an artist's paradise.

I stepped forward, my fingers grazing the wooden handles of the brushes, the cool metal of the palette knives. I could already feel the inspiration bubbling inside me, my mind racing with possibilities.

"This," Eros whispered against my shoulder, "is where you belong. Creating. Bringing your vision to life. You're an artist, April. But not just any artist. You have a way of seeing the world that no one else does. You see it with your heart."

His words sent a shiver down my spine, his lips brushing lightly against the skin of my neck. I swallowed hard, trying to focus, but it was impossible to ignore the way his touch made me feel—seen, understood, wanted. I had never seen myself the way he saw me, as someone capable of creating not just art, but emotion, connection, something deeper.

I let my hand drift over the various supplies until I stopped at the acrylics. There was something about the bright, fast-drying colors that always called to me. Some artists didn't like them—said they weren't as rich as oils or as classic—but I loved the immediacy of them. "Acrylics are underrated," I said softly, running my thumb over the paint tubes. "Oils take so long to dry. I don't have that kind of patience. But acrylics? They let you feel the colors right away, let you see the vibrancy in minutes."

Eros smiled, watching me with that intense gaze, as if absorbing every word. "And that's how you paint your tarot cards?"

I nodded, feeling the familiar buzz of excitement as I thought about the cards. "Yeah. I use bright colors to capture the emotions of each card. The meanings are what drive the art—the feeling that comes from pulling the card, from interpreting it. I want each one to make people feel something."

As I talked, I squeezed a few colors onto my palette—bold reds, deep blues, soft purples. The Lovers card. The idea struck me all at once. I would paint this moment, this place, this impossible connection I felt to him.

"The Lovers," I began, dipping my brush into the paint. "It's all about balance, about union. Two people coming together, but not just for romance. It's a deeper connection—physical, emotional, spiritual.

It's about choice, too. Choosing love, choosing to open yourself up to something bigger than yourself."

As I spoke, I began painting the canvas, capturing the floating island, the sky with its swirling rainbow colors, the marble temples in the distance. I painted two figures—one, a woman with her arms outstretched, her heart open. The other, a man, his hands gently cupping her face as if he were cradling her soul. I wanted to capture the way Eros made me feel—like I was seen, truly seen, for the first time in my life.

He stood behind me, his fingers brushing lightly over my arms as I painted, and I could feel the heat of him. Every stroke of the brush felt like a release, like I was pouring my heart onto the canvas. I wasn't just painting the Lovers card. I was painting *us*. The love I felt for him, overwhelming and impossible.

"I don't have a name for the deck yet," I murmured, my breath catching as his lips grazed the back of my neck. My skin tingled where his mouth touched, and I could barely focus on the painting in front of me. "Nothing has felt right."

Eros was silent for a moment, his hands now resting on my hips, his presence grounding me even as my pulse raced. "What if you called it *The Heart's Journey*?"

I stopped, the words sinking in like they had been there all along, waiting to be spoken. I turned to look at him, the brush still in my hand, and nodded. "That's it. That's what it should be."

He smiled, his eyes dark with something that felt like understanding. "You're creating something beautiful, April. And it's not just the art. It's you."

Hours passed in a blur as I continued to paint, the conversation between us flowing as easily as the strokes of my brush. I told him about each of the cards I'd already painted—The Fool, The Empress, The Tower—explaining how I tried to capture the energy of each one, the emotions they stirred. Eros listened with rapt attention, occasionally asking questions, always encouraging me. His hands never left me—light fingers tracing my arms, my back, my waist. Every touch sent a thrill through me, the chemistry between us palpable.

As I painted, I felt the heat of him behind me, his body so close that I could feel the warmth radiating from him. I was flushed with the attraction, my body buzzing with the need for him, but at the same time, I felt more inspired than I had in years. It was a heady mix of passion and creation, both feeding into each other.

"You paint with so much emotion," Eros said, his voice soft in my ear as he kissed the curve of my neck. "I can feel it in every stroke."

I swallowed, trying to focus on the canvas as his fingers lightly skimmed over my hips, pulling me closer. "I— I try to capture the meaning of each card.

The emotions they bring out in people. That's the whole point, right? To make them feel something."

"And what do you feel when you paint this?" he asked, his lips grazing my shoulder, his voice low and dangerous.

I could barely breathe, the sensation of his touch making it impossible to think. "I feel... everything."

The painting in front of me was nearly complete. The Lovers card now showed the two figures on the floating island, bathed in the rainbow light, surrounded by flowers and the impossible beauty of this place. The colors were vibrant, alive, just like the feelings coursing through me. And the love between the figures—their connection—was palpable, almost glowing on the canvas.

I stepped back, letting my breath out in a slow exhale. "It's... it's perfect."

Eros wrapped his arms around my waist, pulling me against him as we both stared at the painting. "Just like you."

I could feel the intensity of him, the way his body fit against mine, the way his hands roamed over my skin, and I knew that this moment, this creation, was the beginning of something far bigger than I could have ever imagined.

CHAPTER
SEVEN

The painting was finished, my hands still trembling from the intensity of it. It was a masterpiece, or at least it felt like one. Every brushstroke had been guided by something otherworldly, something beyond my control. I stared at it for a moment longer, lost in the colors, the shapes, the emotions swirling within the image.

Then I felt him behind me—Eros. His arms wrapped around my waist, warm and strong, pulling me back against his chest. He kissed my neck slowly, each kiss lingering, his lips soft and teasing. His mouth found mine, and just like that, I was lost to him.

I hadn't made out like this since I was a teenager. Who knew it could still be this fun? This electric? I melted into him, surrendering to the way his body felt pressed against mine. We were already naked, never bothering to clothe ourselves after the first time. There was no need for pretense, no need for anything but each other.

His body... I could hardly describe it without my breath catching. He was sculpted, as if chiseled by the hands of one of the great artists. His chest was broad, his muscles defined, every inch of him pure perfection. His dark hair had flecks of sunlight in it, contrasting beautifully against my own red hair. His skin was golden, kissed by some divine warmth, a warmth that radiated into me with every touch.

But this time, I wanted to take control.

I felt empowered, filled with creativity and lust... no, love. It was love, and it was all-consuming. I pushed Eros gently to the ground, my eyes locked on his as I crawled over him. I could see the desire in his gaze, the way his breath hitched as I licked my way down his body, savoring every inch of him.

Then I reached it—his cock. And it was magnificent, long, thick, gloriously veiny, like something only a god could possess. My mouth watered at the sight of it.

I bent down, kissing the tip of Eros's cock, and he sighed, letting out a breath he had clearly been holding. Slowly, I licked up from his balls to the base of his cock, feeling the heat radiate from him, hearing the soft moans escape his lips. My tongue traced along the length of him before I slipped him into my mouth.

Or at least, I tried. He was so big that I could barely fit the head of his cock past my lips. I moved my hand up and down his shaft, my mouth working the tip as best I could, savoring the taste of him.

But that wasn't enough. I wanted more.

Without a second thought, I straddled him, positioning myself over his cock, and slowly began to lower myself onto him. He stretched me, filled me, every inch of him pressing deep inside my wet, aching pussy. I moved slowly at first, taking my time, feeling every bit of him, savoring the way his body molded to mine.

Eros moaned beneath me, his hands reaching up to cup my breasts, his fingers teasing my nipples as I rode him. I could feel the slow build of pleasure deep in my belly, each thrust pushing me closer to the edge. I placed my hand on his chest, using him for leverage, angling myself so that every movement sent waves of ecstasy coursing through me.

His hands moved to my hips, helping guide me, encouraging me to move faster. My body responded, moving with more intensity, the pleasure coiling tighter inside me, spreading to every part of my body.

Then, as if reading my mind, Eros's hand slid between my legs, his fingers finding my clit and rubbing it in slow, rhythmic circles. The sensation sent me over the edge. I screamed, my orgasm crashing over me in waves, my body vibrating with pleasure. The release was so intense that I was sure the world beneath the floating island would hear us—and I didn't care.

Birds scattered into the sky, their wings beating in time with my heart. I was in bliss. The world was my oyster, and I was in love with a god.

"I never want this to end," I whispered, breathless, leaning down to kiss him.

Eros smiled, brushing a strand of hair from my face. "Neither do I," he said, but there was something in his voice. A weight, a sadness. "But it's more complicated than that."

I stilled, my heart sinking at his words. "What do you mean?"

He stroked my cheek, his eyes soft but serious. "Our time here, in the Arcane Room, is limited. It's coming to an end soon."

I swallowed, the reality of it hitting me all at once. "Will I ever see you again?"

"Yes," he said without hesitation. "I don't know how yet, but I'll find a way. I love you, April Psyche Sullivan. You are a breath of light and love, and for the first time in my long, eternal life, I want to know what it's like to be human."

My chest tightened with emotion. "You want to be human?"

He nodded, his expression earnest. "I want to experience everything with you. All the silly human things I've always wondered about. If I find you, will you show me?"

I blinked back the tears that were starting to form. "If you find me, I'll spend the rest of my life showing you what it means to love one person so singularly."

His smile widened, and he pulled me into a kiss, deep and passionate, full of promises. "I love you, April. More than I can put into words."

"I love you too," I whispered, my heart overflowing.

He held me close, his hands roaming my body, our embrace warm and intimate. "I have a friend," he said softly after a moment. "The Sun Goddess. She's an old friend of mine. She might be able to help."

"Help how?" I asked, hope fluttering in my chest.

He smiled, though he didn't elaborate. "We'll find out soon enough."

We kissed again, slower this time, letting the moment stretch out between us. The world felt distant, like it was just the two of us suspended in time. Eventually, exhaustion began to creep in, and I laid my head on his chest, the steady rhythm of his heartbeat lulling me to sleep.

The last thing I felt was his arms around me, holding me close, whispering promises of a future together.

When I opened my eyes, I was back in the white room.

CHAPTER
EIGHT

opened my eyes, and the first thing I saw was the familiar white room. The warmth of Eros's arms, the magic of the butterflies, the sound of his voice—all of it was still vivid in my mind, but now it was gone, replaced by the clean, sterile white that marked the end of my time in the Arcane Room.

I sat up, my heart full, my mind buzzing with everything that had just happened. It was surreal, like a dream I didn't want to wake from. I wasn't sad, though. I had chosen to feel something else—gratitude, joy, a sense of purpose that I hadn't felt in ages. My heart felt so full that it might burst.

Ms. Vesper appeared in the doorway, her calm presence a grounding force. She smiled, her eyes twinkling with curiosity. "How was it? Do you feel inspired?"

I smiled back at her, my whole body humming with energy. "It's exactly what I needed. All of it."

"Good," she said, walking toward me. "You seem different. Lighter."

"I am," I said, standing up. "I could be sad right now, but I'm going to make a different choice. My heart... it feels so full. I still feel him."

Ms. Vesper gave me a knowing nod and motioned for me to follow her. "Let's get you something to take home, shall we?"

She led me back through the shop, the shelves lined with trinkets and potions I'd grown familiar with over the years. At the counter, she grabbed a small tin and placed it in a delicate brown bag, tying it off with a ribbon.

"Inspiration Tea," she said with a wink. "To help you remember. For when you need that extra push."

I took the bag, feeling a rush of gratitude. "Thank you, Ms. Vesper. For everything."

She smiled warmly, and with that, I stepped out of the shop, the cool air greeting me as I made my way down the street. My mind was buzzing with ideas, and the energy coursing through me was impossible to ignore. I had to paint. Now.

But first, I needed supplies. I popped into *Brush & Canvas*, my favorite art supply store. The bell above the door jingled as I walked in, and the familiar scent of paint and canvas filled the air. Ryder, the owner, looked up from behind the counter, flashing his usual laid-back smile.

"Hey, April," he said, his voice smooth and warm, just like Ryan Gosling's—probably because he looked exactly like him. He leaned casually against the counter, his dark hair slightly tousled. "You're on fire today. I can feel it."

I grinned, waving at him as I headed straight for the paint section. "You have no idea."

I grabbed tubes of every color that caught my eye, stacking them in my arms like I was preparing for a creative storm. As I approached the register, Ryder was still watching me with that easygoing charm.

"Looks like someone's in for a busy night," he teased, ringing up the paints. Then he paused, pulling a package from behind the counter. "Oh, by the way, I've got a package for you. Your Knight of Cups, right? Just came in from the photographer."

I blinked, surprised. I'd almost forgotten about the painting. I nodded, handing over my credit card. "Oh, right. Thanks, Ryder."

"No problem," he said as he carefully placed the wrapped package on the counter. Ryder's store offered an art handling service—he'd take care of getting pieces to and from the photographer, packing them, and mailing them back to the artist. I'd been using his service for years, and it was worth every penny. I hated standing in line at the post office, wondering if my work was safely packaged.

43

I paid for my supplies, thanking Ryder for the help. There was a moment of comfortable silence between us before he said, "You know, if you ever need a hand with your next exhibit, I'm happy to help. I've got connections." He winked.

I smiled, amused by his offer. "I'll keep that in mind, Ryder."

We exchanged a few more words of friendly chatter, before I walked out with my arms full of paint and my mysterious package.

When I finally got home, I felt like I was vibrating with energy. I dropped the paint supplies on my work table, practically bursting at the seams with inspiration. But first, I needed a cup of tea. I grabbed the tin Ms. Vesper had given me, inhaling the soothing aroma as I brewed a cup of the *Inspiration Tea*.

Once the tea was steeping, I sat down to unwrap the package from Ryder. I expected to see my Knight of Cups painting, the one I'd been waiting to get back from the photographer. But when the brown paper fell away, my breath caught in my throat.

It wasn't the Knight of Cups.

It was *The Lovers* card. The one I had painted with Eros.

I stared at it, my heart racing, my mind struggling to make sense of what I was seeing. The colors, the brushstrokes—it was exactly as I remembered. Eros, his hand reaching for mine, our bodies entwined in the painting. It was a piece of the magic we had shared. And yet, it was real, right here in my hands.

My head spun. It had all been in my head... right? Or had it?

I didn't need the answers today. What I did know was that I felt amazing. My heart was full, my soul was alive, and I was ready to create. I looked at the painting, a smile creeping across my lips. Thank you, Eros, I thought. Thank you for everything.

I took a sip of the tea, feeling warmth spread through my body, grounding me. My deck was complete. And so was I. Creatively unblocked, filled with love, and more certain than ever that I was worthy of the grand love stories—the kind they write about in books. The kind people spend their whole lives dreaming about.

And I knew... my story was just beginning.

Jax Wilder

Sign up for my newsletter and get a free book today!

https://mailchi.mp/158597581671/jax-wilder

If you enjoyed the Lover's in the Veil, you might enjoy Heartbound Souls from my new Coastal Cupid series.

The SoulSync Implant doesn't just find love; it guarantees it.

Welcome to Coral Cove, where love transcends the ordinary.

Clark never imagined that her search for love would lead her into the arms of someone like Kade—mysterious, alluring, and not entirely human. With her life defined by the shadows, she steps into the unknown with the help of Coastal Cupid's SoulSync Implant, which promises to find her one true soulmate.

But in a town where the lines between realms are as thin as a whisper, finding love is anything but simple. As Clark delves deeper into the mysteries of Coral Cove, she finds herself torn between her past, her present, and a future she never thought possible.

Will she embrace the darkness to discover a love that outshines the stars, or will the secrets of Coral Cove keep her heart bound forever?

ALSO BY JAX WILDER

Coral Cove Series

Sleighed by Love

Harvesting Love

Dawning Desire

Knead You Now

Love Rewound

Perfect Lover Spell

Haunted by Her

Tarot Fantasies Series

The Devil's Temptations

Strength of the Beast

Hanged Passions

Six of Cups

Death's Embrace

Queen of Pentacles

Seven of Pentacles

Ace of Wands

Three of Swords

Two of Swords

Lovers In The Veil

Stand Alone Titles

Pride and Prejudice and Witches

Additional Books by Rainbow Quartz Publishing

Lorelai Hamilton

Encyclopedia of Divination

Encyclopedia of Cryptids

Encyclopedia of Faeries

Tarot Tales and Magic Spells

Teenage Tarot

Arcane In Verse

The Eclectic Witch's Grimoire

Teenage Witch's Grimoire

Find Your Bliss

Tarot Reflection Journal

Tarot Refection Journal Coloring The Tarot

Dream Journal

Miranda Levi

From A Youth A Fountain Did Flow

The Sea Withdrew

A Tear In Time

Mo(ther) Na(ture)

In Orion's Hands

Jackson Anhalt

From The 911 Files

Isla Watts

A Fairy Bad Day

Surprise! You're a Vampire

Gorgeous, Gorgeous, Gorgons

Mork The Handsome Orc

Adopted By Werewolves

Bite Me If You Can

That's The Spirit!

Rose Dawson's Book Journals

My Time With The Fairies

Enchanted Escapades

Enchanted Escapades

Dewey Decimal Diaries

Siren's Songbook

Pride and Prejudice

Bibliophile's Bounty

Book of Books Journal

Pages & Passages Reading Journal

Bookworm's Companion Reading Journal & Tracker

ABOUT THE AUTHOR

Jax Wilder is a passionate romance author hailing from a charming small town nestled in the picturesque Pacific Northwest. With a heart full of love and an unyielding belief in the power of happily ever afters, Jax weaves enchanting tales of love and connection that leave readers captivated.

Jax's novels are a reflection of her commitment to celebrating the magic of love, and her characters' journeys mirror the warmth and happiness she has found in her own life. Join her on the enchanting journey of love, passion, and enduring connection through her heartfelt romance novels.